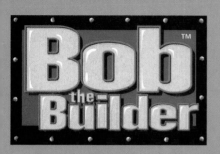

A Christmas to Remember

adapted by Lauryn Silverhardt

based on the book by Iona Treahy

SIMON SPOTLIGHT

New York   London   Toronto   Sydney   Singapore

A snowmobile skidded to a halt outside a house at the North Pole. The radio was sending out a signal. Someone was calling!

The rider jumped off Scoot—the snowmobile—and ran inside. He pulled off his coat and grabbed the headphones off the radio so he could hear the voice at the other end.

"Hello? Hello?" came a familiar voice. "Is anyone there?"

TO: Issac
With Love,
FROM:
Geoff, Aunt Alue,
Uncle Ron

SIMON SPOTLIGHT
An imprint of Simon & Schuster Children's Publishing Division
1230 Avenue of the Americas, New York, New York 10020

Manufactured in the United States of America

First Edition
2 4 6 8 10 9 7 5 3 1

ISBN 0-689-84972-9

The rider flicked a couple of switches on his radio.

"Hello?" said the rider. "Can you hear me?"

"Yes, I can!" said Bob, chuckling. "How are you, Tom? Are you still coming for Christmas?"

"I'm fine . . . and yes, I'm coming for Christmas!" replied Tom.

"Excellent! I can't wait," cried Bob. "See you soon, Tom."

"Wendy!" exclaimed Bob. "I have great news! I just spoke to my twin brother, Tom. He's definitely coming for Christmas!"

"Oh, that's wonderful!" said Wendy.

"This will be a Christmas to remember!" cheered Bob.

"Hey, everyone. I've got some great news," said Bob. "My brother, Tom, is coming all the way from the North Pole for Christmas!"

"Oh, I'd love to go to the North Pole and meet Santa Claus," Dizzy said, sighing.

"I'm sure you will someday," Bob said, laughing. "That reminds me . . . I have to take my Santa suit to the cleaners and we have to put up a tree in the town square."

"And we have to get to the airport . . . ," said Dizzy.

". . . to meet Lennie and the Lazers!" added Roley.

At the airport Roley, Dizzy, and crowds of reporters and fans were waiting for the band.

"What are your plans for Christmas, Lennie?" asked a reporter.

"We're doing a show in the town square on Christmas Eve. Ah-choo!" Lennie sneezed. "I think I'm getting a cold. Let's go to the studio and work on John's new song," he said.

"Wow!" said Roley to John. "Do you write songs?"

"Yes, but the one I'm working on now is pretty tricky," replied John. "Why don't you come with us and watch the band rehearse?"

"Rock and roll!" cheered Roley.

In the forest at the edge of town Bob cranked his chain saw.

"Timber!" called Bob as the tallest fir tree fell to the ground. Lofty picked up the tree with his hook.

"We'll take this back to the town square after we plant these baby fir trees," instructed Bob.

"Why do we have to plant more trees?" asked Scoop.
"To make sure we'll have plenty of Christmas trees in years to come," said Wendy.

Back at the studio, the Lazers were busy rehearsing for their concert.

"Sorry, guys, from the top again," said Lennie. "Aaah-choo!"

"The concert is tomorrow night," said John, worried. "Lennie has a terrible cold, and I haven't even started the new song." John decided to go outside and work on some fresh ideas.

"Hi, John!" called Roley. "What are you doing?"

"I'm trying to write a new song, but it's really hard," said John. "I'd much rather be the singer in the band."

"If it helps," said Roley, "I usually find song ideas from things I see around me."

"Thanks for the suggestion, Roley," said John. "Now, let's see . . ."

Wendy and the machines brought the tree to the town square while Bob met with the new mayor at the town hall.

"Now, Bob," said the mayor, "I'm trusting you with all of the town's Christmas celebrations: The lights need to be put up; Banger, the band's roadie, needs help building the stage for the concert; and don't forget that you're Santa Claus again this year. Can you handle everything for us, Bob?"

"Er, yes . . . I think so," he said, gulping.

Suddenly the tree smashed through the town hall window.

"Oh, no! What happened?" cried Bob as he ran outside. Spud was hanging from the town hall clock by his pants.

"I was helping Lofty with the Christmas tree, but he lost control and the tree went through the window," said Spud. "Help!"

Bob looked up and sighed.

"Now I'm going to have to fix the clock and repair the window, as well as put up the tree and the lights. **Can we do it?**" asked Bob, wearily.

"**Yes, we can!**" everyone shouted.

Back at the North Pole, Tom, Pogo, and Scoot were racing to the harbor to catch the last boat, when a baby reindeer ran across their path.

"Have you lost your dad?" Tom asked. The baby reindeer made a tiny crying sound.

Close by there was a deep hole in the ice. Tom looked over the edge and saw the reindeer's father. He was trapped on a ledge!

"We have to rescue him, Scoot," cried Tom.

Tom used a rope to climb down into the hole. With Scoot's help he hauled the reindeer up.

Once the reindeer were safely together, Tom, Scoot, and Pogo raced off toward the harbor. But just as they pulled up they saw the boat pull away.

"Oh, no!" cried Tom. "It looks like I won't be seeing Bob for Christmas after all!"

After talking to his brother, Bob joined the others in the town square.

"Look, here comes Bob," said Wendy. "He'll help you fix the sound check, Lennie."

But something was wrong.

"Tom missed the boat," Bob said quietly. "He won't be able to come for Christmas."

"That's terrible!" said Lennie.
"Tom lives right up near the North Pole," Wendy explained.
"So he'll never be able to get here in time for Christmas."
But Lennie had an idea.
"Come on, Wendy, to the airport!" Lennie cried.
Dizzy had been listening to Wendy and Lennie.
"I wonder what they're planning," she said with a mischievous look in her eye.

Lennie's private plane landed near Tom's house.

"Merry Christmas, Tom!" called Wendy.

"Wendy? How? Who? What?" said Tom, confused.

"Come on," said Wendy, laughing. "We've got a Christmas party to get to!"

Tom ran inside to get his bag. As he was putting it in the luggage area of the plane, Dizzy popped out.

"What are you doing here?" Wendy asked, surprised.

"Well," said Dizzy. "I thought I'd come along—to meet Santa!"

"Santa will be busy getting his reindeer ready," Tom explained.

"Yes—there's no time to waste," Lennie croaked. "I have to sing tonight."

On the way back Dizzy gazed out of the window.
"Look, Wendy," cried Dizzy. "It's Santa!"
Wendy looked out the window, but Santa had already flown by.
"You've reminded me about Bob's Santa costume," said Wendy. "I said I would pick it up from the cleaners . . . which gives me a great idea."

The sun was setting in the sky as Lennie's plane landed.
Everything was ready for the concert. Lennie joined the band
in the town square. He opened his mouth to say something,
but nothing came out! He had lost his voice!

"Oh, no," said John. "*Now* what are we going to do?"

"Hey, John!" whispered Roley. "This could be your big
chance."

"You mean . . . ?" said John.

"Yes, I do," replied Roley.

"We all agree," said Banger. "You're one rockin' singer!"

Lennie went up on stage first and started the concert by playing his guitar. The crowd went wild!

"Rock and roll!" shouted Roley.

Then John stepped onstage and made his way to the piano.

The first song he sang was the one that Roley had helped him write. It sounded great.

"Yeaaaah!" cheered the crowd.

At the end of the concert Bob suddenly remembered that he was supposed to dress up as Santa Claus and give out presents to the children.

"Oh, no . . . ," he said, groaning.

"Ho, ho, ho!" said a familiar voice close by. Bob stared. Who was this new Santa?

"Merry Christmas, everyone!" called Santa. "And an especially Merry Christmas to you, Bob," said Santa.

Bob looked closely at Santa. "Tom! How on earth? It can't be!" Bob exclaimed.

"Oh, ho, ho. It certainly is!" replied Tom.

The two brothers gave each other a big hug.

"It's great to see you, Tom," said Bob. "But I haven't even done my shopping yet, and it's already Christmas Eve!"

"Don't worry, Bob," said Wendy, chuckling. "It's been taken care of."

Bob felt happier than he could ever remember.
"Thanks, Tom! Thanks, Wendy! Thanks, everyone!" said Bob.
"This is going to be . . ."
". . . a Christmas to remember!" said Tom, smiling.

The End